Wyldsight

Tales of Primal Fantasy

By

Satyros Phil Brucato

Quiet Thunder Productions • Seattle, Washington

Wyldsight: Tales Of Primal Fantasy

This Collection Edited by Sandra Buskirk & Michelle Lunicke
Cover Photograph & Design: Sandra Damiana Buskirk
Cover Model: Zen Klimp
Book Design & Layout: Sherry Lynne Baker

With a Very Special Thanks to Jason Andrew

Published by Quiet Thunder Productions, Inc., Seattle, WA, USA

Printed and bound in the United States of America

ISBN 978-0-9823532-4-0

Publisher's Cataloging-in-Publication

Brucato, Satyros Phil

Wyldsight: Tales of Primal Fantasy : a compilation of stories / Satyros Phil Brucato ; [edit. Sandra Buskirk & Michelle Lunicke]

Summary: Six short stories about feral women, plus author notes and a novel excerpt.

p. cm.

DEDICATION

To Sandi, Coyote, Kelly, Cathi, Inky, Liz, Kristen,
Jennifer, Ann, Heidi, Sonja, Lupa, Zen, Zan, Emily, Danielle,
Cedar, Anu Kelly, and to Wild Girls and Boys in general.
Ah-RHOOOOOO!!!

With a Very Special Thanks to
Zen Klimp, Kelly Klimp, Jason Andrew,
Michelle Lunicke and Sandra Buskirk.

Table of Contents

WAVES

I gave my voice for love, and drowned myself in silence. For him, I walked on knives and left my weightless seas. I bargained with my fear and turned aching eyes toward the sun.

And for this, he left me and gave his heart to someone else.

The song of my sisters calls to me across the waves. I hear the thunder of my father's voice. Alone on shore, I clutch the instrument of liberation in my pale and unfamiliar hands, weighed by the gravity of this new and hostile world. Even in its dimmest light, the realm of my beloved dazzles me near-blind. The roaring of my lost surf haunts me even as I try to sleep. For this love, I have surrendered the swirling comforts of my home. There, I swam with family; here, beheld by eyes of multitudes, I feel exposed. Forsaken. Alone.

For love, I've suffered gladly. And yet, his love belongs to *HER*.

So *rise*, waves! Churn to froth! Pour the challenge of my sacrifice upon his false and freakish kingdom! Flood their streets. Dash their falseness clean. I will *not* melt, not drift away like foam on morning tides. My voice, returned, calls tempests high. Once more, I am a *princess*! Let the people know my song.

ELYNNE DRAGONCHILD

The dark man in the metal dragonskin seized Elynne's arm. She cried out and pulled away. He grabbed her again roughly and shook her, barking words she could not understand. Another armored man laid his hand on the first man's shoulder, speaking to him in soft tones. The first man quieted but kept hold of Elynne, the leather of his gloves warm and sticky with fresh sweat and spilled blood.

Across the vaulted rock chamber, two other men gazed at three charred corpses in smoking armor. They fanned their faces to chase the burnt smells that choked the cavern. Elynne's own gaze blurred and swam. Spilling tears mingled with sweat as she sobbed. Her pained wails echoed through the twisting cavern complex.

The dark man rattled her again. The second man, pity in his gaze, pulled a cloak from his pack and draped it about her bare shoulders. It itched. She shrugged it off. He wrapped it around her again, murmuring a soothing chant. The cloak and the closeness of the two men pressed in, crushing her. A ringing sound rose in her ears.

Not two dozen paces away, a gore-spattered man struggled to rip the heart from the massive dead beast sprawled in its last-stand corner. Elynne's stomach lurched, her legs gave way. The two men caught her as she fell into darkness.

They hadn't even let her say goodbye.

Elynne. Her christened name was one of the few things she remembered from the days before the riders came, sheathed in iron and leather. Barely six summers old, Elynne had slipped away into the forested hills while her village burned. She'd wandered for days, going ever-higher in the hills her people had shunned, and had been near death when the dragon found her.

She had frozen like a rabbit in the dragon's shadow, dropping to her knees in both awe and supplication as it swooped from the sky. The dragon seemed to stretch across the clouds as it landed, blotting out the sun, buffeting Elynne with the blast of its massive wings. Knocked down, stunned on her back, the starving child had felt terror give way to admiration at the majesty of the beast. Its scales shimmered in the autumn sun as the dragon's muscles shifted and slid beneath the armor. Elynne lay transfixed as the dragon's supple neck lowered a massive head down to sniff her, its hot breath snorting like a blacksmith's bellows. Then it withdrew and regarded her with washtub eyes. Despite herself, Elynne giggled as the monster sat back on its haunches like some titanic puppy dog. The creature cocked its head at the unfamiliar sound. After a moment, the dragon reached for her with a monumental claw.

Screaming terror shot through the girl. But days of exposure and starvation had robbed her of the ability to do anything but howl as the dragon wrapped her in its paw and flapped its ponderous wings, rising away from the ground, the trees, the hills where she had wandered. It felt like both dream and nightmare, this flight, and after a while Elynne stopped screaming and simply watched the land spill away beneath the dragon's wings.

The girl had been near-breathless when the dragon alighted at last. It set her gently on the ground before a great cave, and then withdrew its claw.

Fear returned. Would the dragon eat her now? Elynne stood trembling, unwilling to meet the monster's gaze but unable to avoid it. The dragon stared back, waiting, then flicked its head impatiently at the cavern mouth. Elynne started forward, hesitant, waiting for the slash of teeth of a blast of flame. None came. The dragon simply waited.

When she'd reached the stone arch doorway, Elynne stopped cold, unwilling to trespass. The musty air was sweet with the dragon's strangely pleasant scent – a smooth leathery musk, not an animal smell. To the girl's surprise, the creature seemed to nod and grant her access to its lair. She stepped across the threshold, and the dragon unfurled its vast wings again and rose impossibly to the sky. She watched in wonder as it left, and then entered the cave alone.

Inside felt surprisingly warm – a marked contrast to the windy chill outside. A towering hallway narrowed and snaked up a short distance to an anteroom where the smell of smoke and dragon hung like incense in the air. The cavern floor had been worn smooth, and the great walls – sloping upward like the battlements of some fabled city – glowed with a similar polish in the light of a huge fire burning near the center of the room. Smoke from the firepit floated into dark chimneys far above, and smaller passageways twisted off in several channels from the main room.

The stonework, though clearly natural, had been just as clearly carved and smoothed by giant claws and tempered with fiery breath. To Elynne, the cavern seemed like a storyteller's dream world, a faerie kingdom or a playground for elves. But then, wasn't this a dragon's cavern? All the fireside tales the older children had mocked suddenly seemed real, and Elynne's fear and hunger drained away, replaced by a drowsy sense of peace. Whatever the dragon intended, she seemed *safe* for the first time in days. A small stream bubbled from a cleft near the floor, and thirsty Elynne drank her fill. Exhausted, the little girl lay down beside the firepit and slept.

She bolted away to the clack and scrape of claws on stone. The dragon had returned… and with it, her fear. As the monster approached the firepit, Elynne realized that it carried a limp and mangled stag in its nightmare jaws. She screamed. The dragon stopped beside the pit and cocked its head again, paused, and then dropped the stag and quickly rent it to pieces with deft passes of its claws. Being a village girl, Elynne was not so much shocked by the swift dismemberment of the animal as she was by its method. When the dragon plopped chunks of meat to sizzle on the rocks beside the fire, Elynne's stomach roared with hunger.

That night, Elynne and the dragon shared the first of many meals together.

"Tell them to look *harder*! After losing three good men, I don't intended to go away empty-handed."

"Don't let your thirst for gold get the better of you, Fredrick. If nothing else today, we've saved a young girl from the jaws of Satan's hosts. And come through it all *alive*, by the grace of God. Surely that's enough to be grateful for?"

"It isn't that I'm ungrateful, Father, but gratitude won't pay the men or feed the widows. Blast it, the gold must be *somewhere*."

Elynne heard the voices from far away. She could not understand the words, but the tone was clear enough. Hollow pain sang behind her forehead. Sickness tugged at her throat and stomach. She forced her eyes to squint open to the blinding sunlight outside the cave. Wheels creaked. Bridles jingled. Horses snorted. Elynne lay wrapped in soft leather and a fine-spun cloak in the back of a wooden wagon, nestled between sacks that smelled of bread and oil. Groaning, she forced herself to sit up.

Outside the dragon's cave, armored men ran to and fro like ants. Another wagon sat waiting off to her left. A few paces away, the dark-haired man sat high in a saddle while a bald man – the one with the soothing voice – sought to calm the dark one's temper. Hearing Elynne moan, the two men turned to look at her. Elynne shivered. Though she'd held no shame of her body, she felt exposed before these two men's gaze, and so she clasped the cloak in front of herself.

The standing man smiled and spoke gently to her as he moved to her side and drew a sloshing sack from the stock beside her. She stiffened as he clambered aboard the wagon and offered her the waterskin. The dark man dismounted as the bald man coaxed Elynne to drink. She wanted to scream, to spit the stale water in their faces and fling herself at them with a sword in hand and hack them all to pieces. She felt weak and dizzy, though. *Later*, she consoled herself. Later, when her strength returned.

The dark-haired man's voice rang out across the clearing. The man beside her scowled while the first man strutted between the wagons. Elynne's eyes burned as she glared at him. The dark man built to the crescendo of his speech, leaped aboard the second wagon, and whipped the leather tarp from the grotesque trophy underneath.

When Elynne saw the dark man's trophy, she screamed out and was sick.

She had grown up wild and strong after the dragon took her in. As she matured, Elynne had thrown off the clothing, tools and language of mankind. She hunted, fished and foraged with her bare hands, growing accustomed to the weather regardless of the season. As there was no one who could listen, Elynne ceased to speak. She and the dragon did not need words to converse, and in time Elynne forgot what words she had known.

Near winter that first year, and for every year thereafter, the dragon and the girl would build themselves a winter store of food within the caverns, piling up extra wood to keep the fire going. Her guardian would then hibernate through the cold season, leaving Elynne to her own devices. The caverns trapped the heat of the fire and the living earth, and they remained warm all year 'round. During these months alone, Elynne grew bored. Sometimes she would drape herself with fur and wander barefoot in the snow, delighting in the winter's clear, cleansing bite until the cold became too bitter. Other times, she would heft a brand or two from the fire and explore the endless warrens of their home beneath the hills.

In the warmer seasons, all the world was hers to explore. She swam in the lakes and streams, hiked the vast wilderness and scaled the granite hills. She grew strong and brave and self-assured, her hair a wild dark mane. Nothing was beyond her. Each year, she ranged further, dived deeper, climbed higher… and the dragon seemed pleased as she grew to womanhood.

On the day she finally reached the summit of the highest of the hills, she stretched out her bruised and aching limbs and basked in triumph, winds and sun. For leagues in all directions lay unspoiled land, as gorgeous as the dragon or as Elynne herself. As the sun began to color the horizon, the dragon rose and soared above the hills. Laughing, Elynne called to it. The beast circled the mountain she had climbed, eyeing her with concern. Elynne, though, laughed and danced upon the hilltop… and the dragon understood. Fading sunlight glittered rainbows on scales and leathery wings as the dragon capered in the air. Elynne motioned it toward home. With a nod, the dragon flew off across the sunset. Alone, Elynne drank in the sun-washed sights as nightfall came, then picked her way down the hill again in darkness.

She bolted when the wagon struck a rut. The draft horses yelped as the harnesses snapped them to a stop. The wagon pitched forward, and Elynne leapt to the ground. Behind her, men shouted and horses whinnied. She rolled to her feet on the stony turf, flung off the cloak, and ran.

If they'd hit the rut in the forest, she'd have gotten clean away. Even many leagues from home, she knew the woodpaths from long familiarity. But the track the riders had chosen was open, bordered by trees but clear for passage. As she pounded across the naked ground, she heard thudding hooves behind her. She threw herself down and rolled as the dark man rode past her, grabbing at empty air. Another man pulled up short before his horse could trample her. She scrabbled rocks from the earth and hurled them at the riders… but to no avail. They surrounded her, bore her down, and carried her – lashing and spitting – back to the wagons. Against the protests of the bald man, she was bound.

When she was a child, Elynne and the dragon would sometimes play. She found her guardian a willing and gentle, if formidable, playmate with a keen sense of fun and an endless imagination. Yet despite the dragon's power and gargantuan size, Elynne was never hurt beyond the usual childhood scuffs and bruises.

The girl often watched and longed as her adopted parent flew away on some errand or another, remembering her first ride in the dragon's grip. Until she grew older and stronger, however, the dragon refused to take Elynne into the sky again.

As the years passed, Elynne realized that the dragon, though far larger than a cottage in the village where she'd been born, was far smaller than it had seemed when she was young. Back then, it had seemed enormous; as she grew older, though, the dragon appeared to lose some of that forbidding size. Ten summers, more or less, after her adoption, Elynne had grown large enough to straddle the dragon's back. One day, as they played, she grabbed one wing and slipped across her playmate's shoulders. Its cool scales, familiar to her touch, seemed to slide beneath her thighs. The beast rose on its haunches and raised its head to question her. Elynne's heart thundered and her bare skin tingled as she hugged the dragon tighter, willing it to spread its wings and hoist them both into the sky. Tendons tightened and huge bones shifted beneath the dragon's armored hide. Her fingers clenched at scales. She met the dragon's gaze and nodded. *Now.*

Huge wings, furled to the sides, unfolded, lifted, spread, flapped. Elynne's pulse sped beneath her skin. She feared that her hammering heart would explode as her breathing deepened, quickened, then held itself with awe. Clouds of dust and leaves swirled, rose, blew, as both girl and dragon lifted and the ground fell away.

Wind caressed Elynne, whipping hair and rippling skin. She felt her stomach lurch as the trees danced far below. She strained to clutch pounding wing muscles and cobbled dragonhide. Startled birds squawked and wheeled from distant skybourne paths. The air chilled. The clouds approached. A league or so above the ground, the dragon leveled out into a glide. Elynne raised her head, shook the hair from her eyes. Her heart skipped as wide eyes peered down upon the world spread out forever. Not even the highest hill had been anything like this. All below was green and brown. The sun seemed closer, the clouds whisping near enough to touch. Freedom sang within her – the freedom of gods. Vertigo and exultation whirled and warred and stole her breath. Gripping tightly with her legs, Elynne pulled back, sat up, and spread her arms in joy. She sucked breath from the wind that roared in her ears and then bellowed her soul's song. The dragon peered over its shoulder to confirm her safety, but Elynne's eyes were closed and her mouth was wide and her throat sang wordless praise for a long, long time.

Though they rode the skies many times together, Elynne never forgot the first time that she had dared to ride.

The somber hall flickered torchlight. Courtly ladies tittered as Elynne's long fingers fumbled with her eating dagger. The stench of animals and unwashed bodies seared through cooked food and rank perfume. The dragon would *never* have tolerated such a stink. Elynne's long gown itched as she fought against tight corsets for each breath of foul air.

They'd brought her to a castle larger even than the dragon's cave. Instead of wild nature or solitude, though, the place was packed with reckless pets and ill-mannered people. They'd forced her body into graceless, scratchy clothes and her feet into graceless, clumsy shoes. They tried to twist her tongue around their words and her deeds around their manners. When she refused, they cuffed her, shouted, or brought strong men in to hold her down. The dark-haired man, Lord, wooed her with gentle words and gifted her with finery. What use, though, was flattery or finery to a girl who'd ridden naked on a dragon's back? Elynne loathed him. His new-found honeyed manner felt insulting to her honesty. The other people clearly thought her mad, and they treated her accordingly... though with caution and restraint. From daggered looks and appraising glances, she guessed that they found her beautiful. Dressed, though, in their clothes and weighed down by their stone castle walls, she felt ugly and alone. Only the bald one – the one they called Father – could soothe or cheer her... and just a little even then.

Now she sat at Lord's table, blushing at the chuckle of fancy ladies and their servants. Two hands' worth of days and nights following their arrival at the castle, a crowd of strangers packed the banquet hall. Elynne had been wrapped in stifling gowns and led to the table. As she'd entered the room, Lord had bellowed some speech or other and the assembly had cheered. "Smile," said Father – one of the words he had taught her. Stiffly, she obliged. Then came the food, and the fumbling, and the mockery. Father tried to scold the snickerers, but Elynne didn't care.

The banquet was torture.

After too much eating, drinking and suffocating shame, Lord leapt upon the table and addressed the crowd again. Elynne couldn't understand his words, but knew that he was bragging again. She sighed. Lord bragged a *lot*. At length, he clapped his hands and hollered. Two servants came in, dragging a small but sturdy cart. Elynne stopped chewing as Lord strode, jaunty, to the cart. Her throat clenched around the food.

She shuddered.

Lord reached for the drape.

She tried to tear her eyes away, and could not.

Lord gripped the drape and pulled.

The crowd gasped.

Elynne choked on her food, and screamed.

The dragon's head had been mounted on a huge wooden shield covered in the dragon's own skin.

Elynne spat food, grabbed her eating dagger, and flung herself, shrieking, at Lord and his trophy.

The table tumbled as she jumped upon it. Food flew in all directions. Guests screamed and guards scrambled.

She thrashed to her feet and dashed toward Lord, holding the dagger high. Father grabbed for her and missed. Lord stumbled back in surprise as guards rose in Elynne's path.

One blocked her with his halberd. The other clouted her with a heavy mailed fist. Elynne, though, had wrestled with a dragon's claws and tail. Their blows, to her, meant little.

She swung the blade. Felt it bite into mail. One guard cried out. The other dashed her across the wrist with the butt of his weapon, knocking the dagger from her grasp.

Other guards grabbed at her arms and shoulders. From behind her, she heard Father crying out. Now he stood before her, shaking her, pleading while the guards pinned her arms behind her back. Elynne's vision reddened and swam. Strong as she was, she was helpless now. Lord's voice bellowed as he pointed to the corridor.

The guards bore Elynne away while Father followed, begging at her with his soft, soothing voice.

Only once had Elynne roused the dragon's anger. Being long-lived and wise, such creatures had near-infinite patience. A growing, willful child, though, could tax even a dragon's calm… as Elynne had quickly learned.

Once, and only once, she had refused to bathe. The dragon's finicky nose could not tolerate uncleanliness, and her guardian had insisted from the first that she bathe as regularly as the dragon did itself. That day, though, Elynne chose to test her limits as children will. She threw a tantrum, yelling and kicking and refusing to budge.

The dragon remained unmoved.

When Elynne started to run away howling, the dragon merely stepped into her path. She spun around, but again the dragon blocked her.

She stood and shouted. The dragon paid no attention.

She kicked its foot, and hurt her own.

She burst into tears and slammed herself to the ground.

The dragon waited.

She rose and stalked away.

It blocked her again.

She stood firm.

The dragon scooted its paw across the ground, pushing her gently toward the pond.

Snarling, the child picked up a rock and pitched it at the paw.

It bounced off.

She heaved a larger one.

No effect.

The dragon lowered its head to glare at her.

She threw another rock at the dragon's eye.

It connected.

The dragon whipped back its head in pain. The sudden shock tossed Elynne to the ground. Horrified, she watched the dragon thrash its head in tearful agony.

Then it stopped.

Blinked.

And turned again to her.

She blanched with terror.

The dragon growled.

The sound would have sent an entire village trembling.

Fire burst from its flaring nostrils. Tears welled in its eye. The dragon's huge jaw dropped open, baring teeth half as large as the child herself.

Slowly, deliberately, the dragon raised its talon and lowered it over the whimpering child. Just as slowly, it tightened its grasp. To the dragon, its grip was tender. To Elynne, the dragon seemed to crush her.

Child in hand, the dragon hobbled to the pond's edge and then lowered both claw and child into the pool. Then it shook her, pulled her out, put her back under, and then shook her again. Several shakes and submersions later, the dragon released the clean and chastened child on the pool's rock edge, glared at her again, and stalked away.

Elynne never again dared the dragon's anger. Strong and stubborn though she might be, her guardian was unstoppable. Or so she had believed.

The courtyard outside the tower window was quiet now. The revels had ended, and everyone seemed to be asleep, save the night watch. And Elynne.

Inside the room, the finery was dashed. The guards had locked the door, and Elynne had let fly her rage on every object in the room. Even Father had wisely stayed away. She had shredded her gown and the strangling underthings, and hurled the clattering shoes out the window. Hours later, all was quiet.

Elynne sized up the climb from the window to the cobblestones. It was far steeper than the rocks she had climbed at home… but better death now than continued misery. She waited until the watch passed by, then lowered herself out the window, trying a fur wrap about her waist for later use. Hugging bare flesh to cold, rough stone, she recalled her mountain climbs in darkness as she sought toe-and-finger holds. Every floor or so, she would rest and flex in a window crevasse. She reached the courtyard without incident and crept stealthily toward the castle walls.

Once, twice, she ducked the approach of passing guards, moving and freezing like a forest hunter. At length, not long before dawn, she reached the battlements.

She padded to the top of the stairs, then froze.

Father stood not far off, gazing from the wall to the distant hills. He glanced over his shoulder at her and then quickly averted his eyes.

Elynne stood, wary, and then approached the wall – if need be, ready to strike. Father whispered to her, but she understood almost nothing of what he said. Then he sighed and turned to face her, ignoring her nakedness as if she had been clothed. She spread her hands and tried to explain herself but could not find the words. In Father's eyes, however, she saw that she didn't need to.

"Go with God," he said, and that much she understood.

She nodded, gauged the distance between herself and the moat, and leapt.

During the endless winter months, Elynne had laid claim to many passages and rooms within the caverns – many of them too small for the dragon to enter. There, she often entertained herself by drawing on the walls with burnt wood, sharpened sticks and home-made dyes. Chipping impossibly gorgeous designs from the raw stone, she shaped nooks into the caves that only she could fit into or find. Those rooms became her refuge, task and treasure.

The men who'd killed the dragon – her protector, playmate and friend – had scoured those passageways but left them disappointed. According to the childhood tales she had remembered, dragons were supposed to hoard gold, jewels, and other riches. Her dragon had kept none of those things. And so the men took its head, hide and foster daughter as their prize.

But the dragon *had* left a treasure... one all the men had missed. And now Elynne set off for home to claim it from a painted room set deep within the hills.

She traced their path from memory, skirting villages and towns as she went, living off the land as she had since childhood.

Nearly three seasons later, she returned.

A strong scent of old decay greeted Elynn's homecoming. She tossed aside her walking stick and what was left of the ragged wrap, and then descended, trembling, into the cavern. Fading dark stains marked the way.

Tears spilled, but she kept on walking.

Grief hit her as she entered the largest room, burning worse than dragon's fire. The tattered carcass lay ravaged by killers and scavengers alike. She dashed across the smooth stone floor and fell sobbing at the dragon's side.

She wept for a very long time.

Rising at last, she swept the tears away and turned her back on the remains. The firepit, too, was cold and dead. She returned to the surface and retrieved a stolen tinderbox from a makeshift pocket in the discarded wrap. Gathering deadwood, she built a small fire, lit a torch, and carried both wood and torch inside. She re-lit the firepit and built it up with winter-stock wood. Then, carrying a large brand, she went off in search of the painted rooms.

A handful of seasons past, the dragon had taken Elynne aside and led her to its treasure. In the silent way they had shared, the dragon asked her to hide the treasure. Elynne, shaken by both the honor of the request and the nature of the treasure, agreed, and soon buried it beneath the dirt floor of her favorite painted room.

As she reached the room, she found the floor disturbed, the treasure missing.

Brittle fragments littered the floor.

Had she been too late?

Desperate, Elynne searched the room, then followed the tracks upon the floor.

She traced them through the corridors to a refuse heap in a crevasse where she'd tossed winter food remains. Falling to her knees, she dug through sharp-edged bones until she found what she had sought.

The hatchlings grumped and whined as she uncovered them from their hiding place. She figured they were hungry. Even now, each one proved to be a heavy armful. Still, Elynne hauled them both out to the largest chamber and set them by the fire.

It was cold outside.

But as darkness fell, Elynne set off to hunt.

As the dragon had done for her, so she would do for the dragon's children. And perhaps, if she lived long enough, she might even ride the winds again.

CHASER

"We've got to talk."

Gerald's words held an ominous chill. Rachel glanced up at him as they walked. His eyes seemed cold and distant as the San Francisco mist. *Here it comes*, she thought. She'd seen it coming, but felt no better for the knowledge.

He quietly refused to meet her gaze, but looked off into the fog. The sheen on his face reflected the orange glow of streetlights. Up above, a slice of moon glowed fuzzy in the sky. Finally, he spoke. "I think that it may... we might... maybe we shouldn't see each other like this anymore."

A blow prepared for hurts just the same. Rachel swallowed. For a long time she said nothing, just felt the damp sand shift beneath her feet.

They walked in silence for a time before she answered. "Just like that?" The words grated in her throat like glass. Gerald nodded. He had no answer. Rachel hadn't expected him to. "Well, this certainly comes out of nowhere," she said, but she was lying. She thought she knew exactly where it had come from.

"Stand by the fire!" His eyes shine in the bonfire glow, flat and lambent as an animal's. His shirt hangs open, sleeves rolled up. Each curl of body hair catches that light and casts it back at her, gold slivers on dark skin. Their packmates, restless, pace and pose. Rachel meets his eyes, drops her gaze and shuffles forward in the sand, legs thick as iron bars.

Around her, wolves and people prowl, sand flecks glittering in their fur and skin. Some, curious, crouch forward as she steps toward the flames; others look away, grooming themselves or nuzzling one another in mock boredom. Feral malcontents, just another San Franciscan tribe… though wilder, perhaps, than most. Bandannas and dreads, young faces perched on age-worn leathers. Raw as saplings with old-man eyes. Holy sinners on the edge of the sea.

Her mentor, Beth, stares hard at Tanglewood, lean Alpha of their pack. Beth's eyes glare but her lips stay closed. She knows her place and will not speak.

Fury ripples through Rachel's skin. Again she raises her eyes to his. Won't look away. Salt air swirls with woodsmoke and prickly musk. Not far off, waves slide in, whispering. Rachel's voice catches in her throat. "This is bullshit…"

"Quiet." Soft but with the snap of command.

The rich scent of him darkens with anger. It hums in her nostrils, seeps to her bones. Each strand of familiar hair shines across his skin but now he stands distant, refusing to touch. Her toes brush sea-smoothed stones, their surface warmed by the fire they surround. Her fingers flex, their knuckles cracking in the stillness.

No one moves.

"Songchaser," he says at last, "choose."

Rachel swallows but won't look down. Beth had named her "song-chaser" as a friendly poke at Rachel's awful singing voice. The heart-name held a sense of Pack. Each one among them had a name like that. Beth went by Runnerwolf, Chuck by Tailspin, Aliea by Singefur because she sat too close to their fires. The others' day-names remained hidden from her, one more step of separation between their human world and this netherspace they shared. This shelter of impossible grace.

"Choose what?" She hates the weakness in her voice.

"Whether you're with us," he says softly, "or alone."

"So," she asked Gerald, "how long have you been thinking about this?"

"A few weeks." Gerald, oblivious, walked beside her, searching the night mist for answers.

"How long?"

"Over a month," he admitted.

Rachel glanced up sharply. The pack had ditched her three weeks earlier. "Any particular reason?"

He shook his head. "Lots of reasons. I can't put them into words."

"How about trying?" She looked at her feet, sticky with sand, as they walked. Doubt, fear, fury swirled up the back of her throat and burned. Eyes closed, she bit her lower lip. "I need answers."

They walked for a while, no one speaking but the waves.

"I haven't felt too good about us lately," he admitted. "It's a lot of little things."

"So you said." Feral things surged beneath her skin. "Care to be more specific?"

Garlic fear-sweat buzzed between them, drowning out the sea.

"Look," he said, stopping, "we're pretty young, okay?" This was true; Rachel was just shy of twenty, Gerald slightly older. "Let's be real," he continued, "things never last at this age." At her silence, his voice rose tight to a whine. "I still want to try college after all, and I don't want to go to U.C. Berkeley. I just wanna go somewhere else."

"And leave me here." Was she whining too?

"You never needed me to take care of you or anything," he shot back. "You'll find someone else."

"So will you." Rachel started walking again. She felt scabs pulled off deep inside, and the cuts still felt raw underneath. The blood from her lip tasted good. "Bastard," she muttered. Gerald didn't answer, and they walked again in silence for a while.

"Well," she demanded at length, "don't you have anything else to say?"

He shook his head and extended his hand. She refused to take it. "Rachel," he implored her, "don't be this way…"

"What way?" Her words tasted bitter. "Was there some other way I was supposed to take being dumped?"

"I'm not…" he started, then trailed off. "I guess not. No."

"I saw it coming, you know" she snapped, staring at the sand. Pinpricks sizzled on her skin. "I did. I just want a reason. I want an explanation. After almost two years, I think I deserve one." She raised her eyes to his. Gerald flinched. "*Why* are you doing this?" The question held a plea for some normal, rational, human reason. She said it knowing that Gerald had no answer, but wanting one regardless.

His helpless shrug said more than words could say.

She'd met Gerald a few weeks after first waking up naked eight miles from home, with blood in her mouth and wolf-musk clinging to her skin. Before Beth and Tanglewood had appeared in her life, he'd been there at Cindy's party, spotting this cute wreck of a girl curled up in the corner alone. There'd been shitty wine and sloppy kisses and her eyes had been swollen from crying. Gerald touched her shoulder and asked, "Hey, there – you okay?" Rachel had always been a bad liar but she'd refined it to an art form since that night.

He'd been a sweet guy then, cute and awkward, too polite for his own good. It was always easy to keep her temper around him, and he accepted everything she told him with quiet deference. Her packmates, even in their human guise, made him nervous but Gerald never complained to her. He'd drifted past them, ignored their stares, won them over with calm acceptance. Rachel built a house of deceit to shield him from her life, and had kept him as a barrier against the wolf. Gerald was soft in a good way, a comfortable anchor, and she felt freer with him than she did with the pack. Their walks on the beach became a ritual, a cleansing of her spirit. He'd stood at the gateway to her humanity, grounding the woman that the wolf could not command.

Now his voice felt ocean-cold and his eyes were hard as glass.

He stopped and turned away, looking out into the endless dark. Waves rumbled and hissed just out of sight. Mist danced across the slivered moon. "I'm not sure where we're going, Rachel," he said after a while. "We've been together for a long time, but I don't see where we're going."

"That's a lot of crap." Her tone was quiet and sharp. She restrained sudden urge to shove him in the water and scream out the fury just beneath her words. Deep below her skin, Rachel felt other, darker urges. Something inside her twisted and uncoiled. Sensing it, he stepped back. She pursued him, caught by fury and instinct.

Sea air blossomed with hunting scents.

Rachel snarled. He backed up further. "Don't give me that shit, Gerald." The words grated in her throat. "I know you too well." She met his fearful eyes, her own stare predatory-flat. "Be straight with me," she purred. "Is there someone else, or are you just bored?"

Her words stung. "*Fuck* you! This isn't easy for me—"

"Well it's a real treat for *me!*"

"You don't—"

"No, I *don't!*"

"*Listen!*" he shouted. Their eyes locked.

A thick pulse, beating.

A moment, a surge where she thought perhaps he might rise to what she needed.

Then:

"You're asking," he said softly, "for something I don't have."

Gerald glanced down to the sand. "There's nobody else, Rachel," he added, "no. I just… Feelings don't always make sense. We can't…"

He slumped. "I have to go. I'm sorry."

You will be, said the wolf.

"I get this hierarchy thing and all," she says. "It's really just not me."

His mouth twitches. "You don't know what's 'just you' yet. That's the problem."

"It doesn't have to be." She spreads her hands, placating. "Look… Jesus, we're people, right? Not animals—"

"Wrong!" he snaps. "People ARE animals. Especially us. Especially YOU. That's the part you don't want to understand." He smells now like an animal – an angry one. "You're still too young to wrap—"

"Y'know, I'm truly sick of hearing that."

Even the sea holds its breath.

Rachel doesn't catch the hint. "You keep telling me how young and stupid I must be and that's just fuc—"

She can't see him move until her feet clear the sand.

Lean muscles hold her easily at arm's length. Rank musk boils between them. Strong fingers choke the words in her throat.

He pulls her close enough to smell the wolf on his breath. Flat red shimmers in the back of his eyes. His snarl sets her hair on end.

She swallows hard, drops her gaze to the sand and closes her eyes.

He drops her at the fire's edge. Steps away.

Behind them, the others stir. Beth rumbles at the back of her throat. Singefur yelps and draws back. Shapes move in the dark mist, shifting in the sand like phantoms.

His nails rake slow across her scalp, gentle but still sharp. She shudders in the fire-warmed sand. Her hair follows his stroke, caught in his nails, falling strand by strand.

The last one drops. He draws his hand away.

"Without rules, without structure" he says, softer, "we're creatures of confusion. Without them, we don't know when to bite and when to hide. Our limitations keep us safe. Until you realize that, Songchaser, you're a hazard to us and to yourself."

"Give her more time." Beth's voice rustles just above the waves.

"She's had time," Tanglewood replies. "See how much good it's done."

"She's a kid—"

"We can't afford 'kids'." His words catch the sea's cold finality.

"Meaning what?" Rachel's voice feels dead against the sand. Opening her eyes, she looks toward Beth.

"Meaning we won't kill you," Tanglewood replies. "Not yet, anyway." Beth's strained expression shows this decision was a near thing. "Still," he continues, "you can't stay. Not like you are. Not with us."

She rolls over to face the Alpha Wolf, careful now to avoid his eyes. "I thought you said I had a choice."

He stiffens. "You did. You just blew it."

She shuts her eyes, bitter. "Fine. So who am I with now?"

Again, his mouth twitches. "Both sides of yourself."

The wolf inside her reared its head. Rachel felt its heat behind her eyes. It bared its teeth and she fought to drive it down again.

Gerald took her silence for speechlessness and reached for her.

"Don't!"

He flinched. Rachel's vision sharpened. Her heart jumped. The mist around him seemed brighter, seen now through predatory eyes. The taste of Change, like a mouthful of summer grass, rose sudden in her mouth. A voice inside her screamed *Not now!*

A strong gust blew in from the sea, biting through her damp jeans and leather jacket, raising goosebumps on her skin. She shivered, but the thrill went deeper than a random breeze. She snarled.

Gerald met her eyes.

She pinned him in place without raising a hand.

With fur and spit, seawater and blood and red silk cords, they bind her. She struggles underneath their grip, held down to cold sand while Beth whispers in her ear.

There's wet fur between her fingers, fear-musk in her lungs, panic crying in the back of her throat and rage clawing through her gut. His words blur, meld together and sink beneath the waves.

They cut shapes into the sand. Arrange the stones in black circles around her. Paint her face with bloody lines, one splitting it straight down the middle.

Above them, the misty moon hangs like a judge.

"Wolf and woman are not one within you." The chant rings heavy in their human throats. "Two hearts war 'til one heart wins." The wolves croon counterparts as Rachel sobs. "No breath share you among us," the chant continues. "Run too free, run alone."

The Alpha plants his foot in the middle of her chest, his rangy weight pushing her into the sand. "Turn your head."

"No."

"Turn your fucking head or lose it!"

"Rachel…" Beth warns. "Please…"

Tears blind the girl. Finally, she bares her throat.

Tanglewood nods, face hard, eyes luminous. He stoops to gently brush a bit of sand from her cheek, then presses his hand beneath her chin.

A faint growl. Beth lowers her head, eyes staring straight at Tanglewood. A wash of something – sadness? regret? – passes over his face. Again, his mouth twitches in one corner. He looks down at Rachel and softly closes his eyes.

With implacable slowness, he squeezes his fingers across her throat. The others croon a single tone. "Songchaser," he speaks with ritual precision, "we send you out. Until you walk with a single stride, until you feel the call of the pack, until you calm the storm in your heart, we cast you out to walk alone."

The packmates, save Tanglewood and Beth, turn their backs on her. Tanglewood hesitates, shakes his head and, shoulders rigid, shuts her out. Beth lowers her gaze to the sand, closes her eyes, and joins them.

Rachel looks up at their flame-washed forms, seeing only the rough sympathy of wolves.

She'd wandered the park for hours after the rite, daring strangers to hassle her. No one had. When she reached home, her rage built to a fever pitch. Clenched rigid by sheer will, she paced the hardwood floor, muttering to herself until the dam broke inside and she snatched the first thing that came to hand — an incense burner shaped like a Chinese Fu dog — and hurled it against the mirror. The bright smash sent her into a frenzy of destruction, ripping furniture, trashing knickknacks, baying in rabid fury.

The wolf had her in its jaws. Its rage shredded everything in sight.

Her fury spent, she sagged, weeping, to the floor. Her clothes hung in tatters. Mirrored glass bit into her knees. Blood welled up with tears. She cried until she couldn't breathe, then reached at last for the phone.

When Gerald came, he asked no questions. Only held her 'til she finished shaking. He whispered words that meant nothing, stroked her hair, cradled her in too-thin arms. When Rachel finally calmed down, he helped clean up the mess, his brown eyes clouded with concern.

"Rachel?" Gerald's eyes were wide, his voice uncertain. The wolf in her wanted to rip those eyes from his head. It would be so easy, here, alone, to share her pain with him. Words, bloodlust, torrents of fire and much, much worse seethed too close for safety.

"Go home, Gerald," she muttered, breaking eye contact and turning away.

Was he to blame? Would this have happened without the pack's exile? Did the problems between them run deeper than deed or ritual, below the surface of things they'd never said? Should she blame Gerald? Tanglewood? The pack? Herself? *Think about it, really*, she mused, and settled on herself. *If you're honest*, that voice continued, *you know damn well who to blame*. Her belly boiled with recrimination stew, seething and shifting like greasy red soup. It bubbled up the back of her throat and peppered across her tongue.

Honesty? That's fucking rich. Where should she begin? *I'm a werewolf? I'm alone? I hate myself for loving you and I hate you for letting me do it? Yeah, sure – let's go THERE now.* That'll *work…* Honesty was a leg-hold trap, one she'd chewed limbs off to avoid. Rachel had built a wall of lies – to her pack, her lover, herself. Didn't they *both* do that, though? Didn't *everyone?*

Even Tanglewood, with his precious integrity, lied his ass off when it suited him. So what lies had *Gerald* maintained? What truths had he kept to himself? He knew so little about her, really – how little did she know about him in return? What went on in his head when Gerald stopped talking? Two years gone, and far too many lies.

She thrashed around cages in her skull. Her gums ached as they drew back tight. Locked teeth sharpened behind her lips. Any words were the wrong words. Rachel shook the thoughts away. She hurt too badly to think this through. Better puzzle through it later, when the wounds weren't quite so raw. *Get away now. Heal.* Maybe a party. Maybe a drink. Maybe a run past the end of the world.

"Hey, wait," Gerald called as Rachel walked away. "We can talk about this!" Now he was beside her, reaching for her arm.

She pulled away. "There's nothing to talk about. You've said enough. Just go."

"Hey, look – I'm sorry."

"So am I, Gerald. Leave me alone." Hurt lodged in her chest like glass. "For your own good, go home."

"Is this it?"

"That was your decision." The wolf gnawed at her self-control. Pain and loneliness, rage, confusion, sadness washed through her like ocean waves. Had she loved him, ever? Did she *now?* Too many questions, too many doubts. "Please just go."

She'd sensed the difference in Gerald after that. The half-hidden glances when he thought she wasn't looking. The stale drift that smelled like fear. No questions, though. Ever. He hadn't asked her what was wrong. He simply withdrew, like the pack but without their anger. Roughly three weeks after that crazy night, he'd cast her out as well. Was this the pack's doing, or Gerald's, or her own?

"I'll take you home." He reached for her again.

"*Go!!!*" She lashed out, spun. He cowered from the wolf in her eyes.

Change bristled just beneath her skin.

Rachel stepped forward. Her prey stumbled backward, sprawling in the sand. The fear in his eyes dimmed as she blocked the light, throwing her shadow across the sand. She smelled his sudden sticky fear. Her fingers curled into hooks, claws itching to extend. Her teeth throbbed. Sharpened into fangs. Shards of humanity kept her claws from his throat. Flickers of will kept the wolf inside.

"*Get out of here.*"

Gerald scrambled to his feet, eyes rabbit-wide. Rachel trembled, wanting to hug him, wanting to kill him, and turned away instead.

Striding waist-deep into the freezing surf, she forced the wolf back down. Cold waves slapped her. Crashed against her legs. Drenched her belly. Soaked her chest. Sent her shivering.

Rachel waited there, hugging her sides until the fury stilled. When she turned around, he was gone.

She howled until her throat went raw. The sound got lost in the roaring surf.

They strain: wolf and woman, struggling. Red cords burn across their skins, biting deep enough to bleed. Rich scents coil as they breathe, reaching in and drawing out again.

The wolf thrashes in her grip. She dodges its teeth and wrestles it down. Locking eyes, they snarl. The sound becomes one with the ocean's roar.

It pulls her, draws her, taunts her, dares her.

Furious, she dives...

Thrashing, spinning, no air, no light. Cold weight, dragging. Darkness. Sand.

Shedding bonds. Shedding leather. Bursting up through cold sharp stars.

Up above, a chill moon glaring. Slivered. Rimmed with fog.

Furious, she sputters. Gasps. Starts to swim. Not toward the beach – away. Toward deep water solitude. To drown? To fight? To escape?

To tear the moon to pieces from its sky.

Sounds boil, wordless fury. Stagger from lungs washed cold with salt. Choke from tight throat howled raw. Burn in boundless frenzy mind.

I will kill the moon, she cries.

Wolf and woman strive as one. Two hearts share a single pulse. Two throats share a single breath.

Storms burst against them, and they fall…

Gasping, Rachel broke the surface. Cold waves shook her like a soggy rag. *What the hell am I doing?!?* Far off, faint stars of orange flickered. Bonfires. The beach. Behind her. She'd been heading out to sea.

Clarity broke colder than the waves.

No fucking WAY! she thought. *Not happening.*

Arms heavy, she chased her way toward shore.

She rose spitting from the surf, drenched and shaky and salty and alone. *God, Tanglewood,* she thought, *you SUCK!* Disgusted, Rachel shook herself. *Lost my jacket. Marvelous.* Still in all… she looked back toward the hungry dark.

Her legs dropped out from under her.

And for a time, she lay numb on the sand.

Hours later, Rachel stood alone on the beach, cleansed by the Pacific wind. Her eyes stung but she refused the luxury of tears. The sliver moon now hid itself, wrapped in mist like a blanketing womb. There was pristine beauty in the night, and both wolf and woman welcomed it together.

Rachel's breath misted near her face. Waves washed across her feet. Breeze soothed the jagged spots inside. Her sadness lingered, but the bitterness waned. *It's about time*, she thought, *for rebirth*.

The wolf and the woman, they'd said, *are not one*. That curse no longer seemed true. After the last few hours, perhaps they'd reached some understanding. They would clean up future messes themselves.

In the raw distance along the beach, bonfires warmed the flickering mist. From one came the sound of drums, laugher and off-key songs mingled with the wash of waves. Rachel paused, recalling similar nights with Gerald, with Beth and Ray, Shelly and the mousy blonde with a name no one could pronounce. Wet evenings in cool fog with beers and fires and old friends. With the pack, even Tanglewood, his fingers light against her skin. Gone now, only memories. She shivered. It was a good night for sorrow… but sorrow was a waste of time. Her life was smashed to slivers, now. Best to bury the pieces and move on.

Down the beach a ways, firelight glittered on a rash of broken glass. Cans and bottles jutted from a blackened mound of sand. Rachel swore as she approached the mess. The campfire embers guttered. Smoke rose into fog. The tracks of the bastards who'd left this mess led up to the pavement and away. By the look of their fire, they were long gone. Pity.

She let out a thick disgusted sigh. "I fucking *hate* when people do that." Folding carefully to her knees, Rachel knelt beside the fire and sifted through the sand. Some asshole had built a beer-can Stonehenge, the metal wet and gritty to the touch. A soggy paper bag held fast-food wrappers and two more cans. The cheap scents grated on her nerves.

Cursing, she threw the first few slivers in the bag. The flat *clinks* matched her mood. She stopped. Thought. Looked back out toward the waves.

Damp fur brushed against her hand.

She glanced down. Nothing there. *Of course not.* Still…

The next few pieces fell softly in the bag.

Sweeping fingers through the sand, Rachel searched for broken glass. Her efforts carved designs, wedged damp grains underneath her nails. As she worked, she thought of Gerald, cleaning up her broken mirror. *I guess I'm not the only one who got stuck with someone else's mess*, she mused. *I guess it's time to clean up my own.*

The larger pieces were easy to find. The hard part involved the slivers, stubborn shards half-hidden in the sand. *No matter how carefully you pick them away*, she thought, *there are always some waiting below the surface. You could sift sand all night and never catch them all…*

But leaving a few tiny shards behind beat large fragments lying around. Given time, the sea would wear the slivers down until shards and sand became one. *'Til then, I guess, you just take your chances and hope no one steps on the glass.*

Her legs had cramped by the time she finished. She stretched and grunted, then carefully raised the bag. The glass inside rustled as she cast a last slow scan across the sand. "You can never," she repeated aloud, "get them all." Rachel brushed damp hair from her eyes with a gritty hand. It was better than nothing, and would have to do.

Off a ways, the songs continued. *Wow*, she thought, *they REALLY suck*! Maybe they could use some company…

Rachel grinned as something settled warm beneath her skin, put its face on its paws and went to sleep.

Dumping the bag in a nearby trashcan, she headed back down the beach to chase a song.

WILLOW & WIND

(For Kristen Leigh Elmore and SJ Tucker.)

Once, as they say, upon a time, there was a tree – a willow standing in a forest on the fringe of the world, far from the woods known by man. And although this willow bent himself near a clean and soothing stream, he felt alone.

Then one day, an errant east wind rippled through the willow's branches. In their rustling and ticking, they wove enchanting songs, and the wind lingered long past the time when a breeze should have passed on. They grew to love one another, the willow and the wind, and beside the stream on the fringe of the world they made precious music together.

But winds are fickle things, and soon the restless breeze blew far and away. Once again, the willow stood alone. Then one day, a young woman stepped up to the tree – a girl in the woods where no human foot had fallen. And she sat in the willow tree's shade, singing familiar songs. She took up fallen sticks and clacked them together. The tree rustled his branches and she whistled her tunes and then she turned back into the breeze and played among his limbs. As the sun set, they made love, and by the light of a waning moon the woman-wind taught her beloved to dream himself into the form of a man.

Filled with bright enigmas and tales of precious lands, they took one another's hands and ventured into the woods. Following the whims of the wind, they crossed strange paths and wove new passages through places without names. In time, they stepped beyond the forest's edge and entered the world of men. The willow trembled and the wind wavered, but soon the lovers found their place in this dense and thorny realm.

For a time, the willow-man and lady breeze prospered in the mortal lands. They played and sang and loved ten thousand human pleasures. The wind shimmered with rare beauty, dawn-haired with sunset eyes. The wind stood tall – lanky, rangy, handsome in a hangdog way. His fingers struck wonders from wood and steel; her voice drew pictures on the contours of each heart. When they played and sang together, people flocked like hungry birds to hear.

But soon the wind grew restless and the tree felt rootless, and when men offered them gold and glorious chains, he refused.

They quarreled then, the willow and the wind. They tossed and they stormed and they broke treasures without price. Their fury scoured walls bare and scattered dreams like autumn leaves. Fathomless with sadness, the willow reached into his chest and broke off a branch from deep inside his heart. He left it on her pillow as she slept. "With this," he whispered, "you will always have our songs. But as long as you wander the world of men, you may have their gold and praise and chains, but you will never again have me." And he left her then, stalking off into man's world to find his way back home.

But man's world grows thick on you, like moss or ivy. All paths seem to become one, leading you back to the place you stood before. The willow soon found he could not find his way back to the edges of their wood. The more he sought them, the fainter they became. Home-songs drew him onward, but each back-alley and dead end chased his path a little further off. Now, it's said, he sits by the edge of a stream, struggling to sing or weep or dream his way back home again. Some folks say he's trying still. And the wind blows empty through the world of man, seeking a familiar touch and the rapture of their song…

GRAMMA WOLF'S GARDEN

Not all wolves eat little pigs or children. Some eat flowers, magic or secrets. You never hear about those wolves, though. They keep to themselves at the far edges of the forest. The moon, for them, is communion enough. A girl's sighs of woe or pleasure can sustain them for weeks on end. Still, it's not wise to trespass there. All wolves have teeth, you know, and a predator of secrets may be the most dangerous kind.

In the perpetual shade of a balenor tree, there's a cottage overgrown with ivy. Though it gives the grave impression of unspeakable age, its windowpanes remain unshattered and its door glows with fresh paint after each new moon. Around that cottage sprawls a garden of such rich proportions that in spring it swells to engulf the house. Its blooms blaze bright as summer lovers, save for those which bloom at night; these trap the graceful shiver of the moon and shine it back in muted hues. No flagstones mark the thick front yard. No axe sticks proudly from its chopping block. Welcome to Gramma Wolf's Garden, where Grandma never died.

Long ago, a woman made her home deep in the forest. She labored hard to build it safe and strong. Her old name has been lost to time, so calling her Gram will suffice. Back then, they say, Gram was vibrant and beautiful; the bloom of each moon's blood still crept between her legs, and she'd grind herbs into autumn-scented powders and then drink them with her tea on the nights when she'd take a strange lover to bed. The widow of a woodsman and the daughter of an herb-wife and a stonemason, Gram had hands strong as winter winds and a heart warm as a crackling hearth. Silver strands peppered the fall of her hair, while eyes the brown of fresh-turned earth caught the laughter of a child and the gloom of a poet with equal measure and grace. She spoke little, but the few words she said fell to the ground and sprouted flowers. Kindly children who picked them sang in their sleep, while spiteful ones tossed whining through dreams of wild hells.

When Gram had been a child, her mother taught her to seed small gardens with sweet whispers; her youthful tantrums wove briars between the flagstones and wrapped rose-vines dense with thorns and black petals among the rafters of their home. As she grew, Gram's mother taught her to speak flattering bouquets and murmur healing herbs into moonlit soil. She sang crops to fullness and gardens to bloom. Gram's reputation blossomed like a rainy-season wood, and when a fever took her mother down, Gram – scarcely more than a girl by then – became the cherished herb-wife in her place.

Not long afterward, Gram met a woodsman with tangled hair and shining eyes. His skin held a sapling's rough suppleness. Sunlight glistened on his bare shoulders. He smiled often and needed few words to gauge Gram's mind or speak his own. Though he'd built his cottage far beyond the village paths, Gram slipped often through the shadowed woods to see him after dark. In the bloom of young love, she'd whisper white havermusk beneath the window of her beloved. Their cries of ecstasy made twigs bud on the contours of his furniture, and filled forest clearings with dazzling red forget-me-nots. On the day they married, every flower for a thousand miles opened in full bloom. The birth of their first and only child cracked trees with the power of her screams. Her husband brought Gram handfuls of long-stemmed honeywine as she nursed their child, and her milk pulsed with the throb of wild life.

Sadly, life is often cruel. Just as Gram's mother and father had died before their season, her husband broke his leg at the bottom of a ravine and perished in a tangle of thorns. A kind-eyed passing wolf heard his cries, crept down into the ravine, and nuzzled the dying man to sleep. As he slipped beneath a soft and endless slumber, the woodsman whispered a promise to his beloved. No man living knows his final words, but the wolf caught them between lupine jaws, licked the woodsman's brow, touched one paw to his forehead as his spirit passed beyond the pain, and then clambered up the edge of the ravine.

When darkness wrapped the cottage the woodsman had built, Gram set out to find her mate. Strapping their child to her back, she had just stepped out on the forester's path when the wolf emerged from the mist. Behind him, a grim pack gathered on the path. Kind eyes shining with sorrow, the wolf bowed his head low to the ground. Gram raised her walking staff high, as if to bash out his brains, but stopped when he would not defend himself or flee. The wolf met her gaze, opened his jaws, and let the woodsman's whispers out. They scattered on the ground like acorns, blossoming into his final words to her. Eyes blurred with unshed tears, she beckoned the wolves into her yard, fed them dinner, and murmured her thanks. Jarrowbone flowers, pale blue and glowing like the moon, grew at the wolf's feet, and from that moment forward Gram, the wolf and his pack remained close as roses and thorns.

People whispered. People swore. Men came from the village
to drive the wolves away. Gram had none of it. She muttered
viperweed at the gossipers and shouted briars at the hunters' legs.
In time, the grumbling townsfolk shunned Gram's cabin. Though
brave market-children still tangled at her skirts and people still
came to purchase remedies, rumors of Gram's wolfpack chased
familiarity from her life like ducks before the sticks of angry boys.

Gram used solitude to weave lush gardens around her home.
Her wolves ate flowers, not lambs, and they basked warm in the
sunlit yard. Strong-nerved customers won themselves an honor
guard of lupine company. No one was ever robbed or injured along
the path to Gram's cottage. The gardens brimmed with herbs and
flowers beyond naming. Some folks claimed that Gram's wolves
paced the village at night, stealing secrets and bringing them home
to bloom. Indulgence curdled into curiosity, into gossip, into fear.
As her son grew toward manhood, Gram's name sent sweet sullen
whispers around the wells and cottage tables of her town.

Those whispers stung Gram's son. A bold-featured boy
whose face recalled his father's ghost, he lacked their family's gift
for nature. He was a shaper, a moulder, a grinder, a hammerer.
Forsaking his mother's garden and his father's ax, the young man
took up the smithing trade. His ears echoed with the pounding
of the forge. His hands tingled with the blows of steel on steel.
His words huffed and clanged with blunt impatience, and the
cottage gardens soon groaned behind stone walls and iron fences.
The wolves snapped at him and he snapped back. What few
words passed between Gram and her son held a ragged edge as he
reached manhood and took a wife.

Gram's son claimed the weaver's pretty daughter as his mate;
Gram, though, had little patience for the bitter-tongued girl. The
wife had no great love for Gram in return, and though the three

shared the cottage Gram's husband had built, its walls soon paled
from the venom of their words. Fence posts bristled with glistening
hooks. Stone walls crawled with restless ivy or abruptly collapsed,
crushing frail shoots and crackling bushes beneath their weight.
Distressed, the wolves fled the garden and feasted on caged lambs
and shrieking cattle. By the time the first grandchild swelled the
weaver's daughter's belly, Gram bundled necessities in a heavy
leather pack, gathered up her wolves, and headed off down a path
thin as treachery through the spring-dappled woods.

Now, these were not the slim and sickly woods at the borders
of man's world. These were the edges of the Old Wood, where
the first seeds of Creation took root and grew. Gram hustled
her bundle and wolfpack through ravines, bore them over rivers,
wrestled them up stark cliffs from which you could see ten
thousand kingdoms at a glance. In her wake, Gram left toadstools
ripe with curses and glens bold with flower-songs. When she spoke
to herself or to her wolves, the syllables blossomed into crimson
stagweeds and spectre-pale widowcrook; when she'd meet a fellow
traveler, her words tumbled to the ground and grew into succulent
fruit. She sang at the birds, dusted the dirt with pollen and
muttered at nothing in particular, leaving briars where she'd stood.
The deeper she went, the more her words flowered. What had been
a strange talent in the village where she'd lived now became a lush
inheritance. Gram loved the Old Woods, and they loved her in
return.

The wolfpack flowed through those woods at her sides, at
her lead, at her heels. The merciful wolf paced beside Gram,
often drifting ahead but never out of sight. Each evening, they
surrounded her, carrying back torn rabbits and ravaged deer
carcasses as she kindled fires and sang up herbs. She tended them,
they tended her, and though all but the bravest living things dashed

off when Gram's pack neared, the season cloaked them in mist, bathed them with cool rains and anointed them with filtered sun.

Four days and three nights out from Gram's old cottage, one clearing finally felt like home. Perched on the edge of a deep pond fed by nearby waterfalls, the moist soil hosted festivals of bright-hued magnificence. Lush spans of bright blue candlemere bobbed their heads in the faint breeze. A rash of violet roses climbed the balenor trees at the clearing's edge. Mist filtered the early morning light, ghost-breath-like and luminous as love. Gram set down her pack, took out her tools, and began to shape the wild to her will. Slowly, day by day, she plied the skills and talents of her family, raising a fine, if tiny, cottage and surrounding it with song-birthed gardens.

Each night at dusk, the kind-eyed wolf came to visit her, bringing gifts of fresh meat and company. Each full moon, Grandma reached naked to the sky, a crone dancing to deep wolfsong. The wolf brought packmates to her clearing and they helped her pray all night. Each morning of those exultations, new flowers bloomed outside the cottage. In no time, they filled the clearing, drawing, in turn, birds and beasts of all descriptions.

But wild places breed wild things… and the wild shaped her, too.

As time passed, Gram grew gaunt and feral-lean. Twigs and thistles wove themselves in her hair. Dirt blackened her fingernails and soles. Woven pelts soon replaced her threadbare clothes. Gram smelled of musk and sweet-turned earth, the herbs she gathered and the beasts she ate. Gram's eyes glowed wolf-shine in the early morning mist. Yet her cottage remained clean, its contours shaped with skilled precision. She swept the stone floors clear of dust, and carved statues out of wood and stone. Filigrees of unknown languages danced across the walls and etched themselves in the earth. Were they warnings? Tales? Enchantments? Only Gram could say.

At times, the ancient presence of the Wood bore down on her with all the pressure years could bear. She awoke some mornings weeping for her son, stirred by dreams of bellies swollen with fresh life. As the seasons turned, Gram envisioned grandchildren sired and birthed in the cottage built by her husband's hands. Her own hands gnarled like old kindling, but her voice stayed strong and her step held the lightness of the girl she'd been. Her wolfpack never seemed to age; like stones, they held time to their breast and watched man's seasons fade.

Once or twice per season, Gram trekked back through the forests toward town, flanked by runner-wolves and her kindly-eyed companion. As she walked, time turned back upon itself, as it so often does in the Old Woods; one trip might last a single day, another passed in an afternoon, and still other trips seemed to last a week or more. Although Gram followed the path she'd blazed, it never ran the same way twice. So long as Gram kept to that path, she'd always reach her destination. Once, in curiosity, she wandered off to form a new path, and then got lost for weeks. It's said that she eventually found the edge of the world, where raw cliffs plunge into nothingness, and might have been lured off the side by the voices of the dead had the kind-eyed wolf not found Gram and led her home again.

Gram never strayed from her path after that.

But solitary woods breed monotony for human minds… and so, she'd wander from time to time back into town, sun-browned skin ripened like old apples and silver hair spilling from her hood. Children ran to cluster in her shadow, plucking flowers of endearments as she bent to rustle their tiny heads. She would trade precious herbs with the merchants in their stalls, fetching salt and tools and cloth to take back home.

Once or twice in these visits, Gram thought she'd seen her son and his family; if so, however, the years had gnarled them both. Where he'd once been slim and strong, the man she saw now trundled with unhappy weight. The viper-faced woman at his side stood thin as parchment, dense with sure unspoken threats. The children crouched at their sides, drowsy monks shorn of the vitality proper children know. Each time, like a pack of sullen monkeys, the family slid into the market crowds before Gram could call out to them. In the thin cover of the marketplace, they seemed elusive as scared deer. Gram frowned at this but refused to chase them. Whispers slipped from her pursed lips, though, and grew thorny flowers where they fell.

Some folk in the village remembered Gram well; others drew back from her presence and held their children close. She was a rumor, a demon, a flicker of nameless dread. Where certain folk smiled, others cringed. Mama Thistle, they called her... or Gramma Wolf.

Gram did not come to the village alone. Though he stayed well out of sight at the borders of the town, the kind-eyed wolf and his pack watched for her return. When she would emerge from the market, heavy with tears and trade-goods, the wolf licked her hand and nuzzled her face and sang wild songs for her. In time, they'd leave the town behind, Gram's footfalls lightening with each league until she walked with sure and feral steps. Each journey into town became a trip through time – a visit back to youth that left her old until she left the town behind and became young again.

Years passed. Trees grew. Children became young adults while their parents soon turned old. Whispers crept out of the woods, settling in hungry ears. Gram, the whispers said, was wealthy, was a witch, was hiding gold beneath her garden's soil. She was younger now, claimed the tales, than her own son was. Back in town, Gram's son and his wife creaked with bitter age. Their own children, thick as mossy stumps, became mirrors of their impermanence.

And so, the son and his wife decided, they would visit Gram in the woods, and coax from her that secret of eternal youth.

Knives and axes struck bright sparks from the whetting stone that night.

The next morning, Gram's son, and his three sons, and a daughter who was more boy than girl all set off to find the path that led to Gram's clearing. They whispered to one another of plans and treacheries. Dull words fell from them like stones, shot through with glimmers of fool's gold and iron red. They hefted sacks and axes, with sharp knives clenched along their belts. Back home, the wife and three more daughters brewed grim bread and razor tea. Their garden rustled thick with worms and dead things left for soil. A stout chair with iron bands awaited Gram's return.

In the woods, the wind caught snatches of the plan, and brought them to the kind-eyed wolf. He ground them between his teeth like bones and then spat them into the dirt.

The ground shook, and the brooks shivered, and the trees rose up their roots to trip the ironsmith and his children. Boots tangled and men swore. Branches wove in tight together, plunging the forest into early darkness. Overhead, the birds cried warnings.

And the pack prepared.

The kind-eyed wolf called his kin. From all across the land, they came – red wolves and black wolves and wolves as gray as slate. They slipped through the woods on ghostly paws.

Gram felt the land shiver, and she howled with despair.

There are winds born on the tongues of mothers, rumbles beneath their bones where new lives begin. The hearthfires of eternity beck and crackle in the wombs of every birthing woman, and their embers never truly still. For Gram, those winds and bones and fires coiled into wordless tears that spilled from her in coruscating streams. Sorrow cracked through her like a whip-strike in still air, leaving Gram bent and shivering in its wake.

Sensing the approaching wolves, the smith and his children struck flint into fire and raised torches toward the meddling trees. Their mouths tumbled curses. Calloused palms and fingers tightened around worn-smooth axe-handles. Their eyes flickered, watching the trees. And yet they walked further into the forest, intent on the treasures of Gramma Wolf.

She saw them through the trees, watched them move along the path, spied on them through leagues of distance through the power of the Old Woods. If she'd willed it, her son and his children would be lost, wandering through the Old Woods until the skin slid from their bones.

Gram considered this.

Watched it in her mind's eye.

Saw days and weeks glide along their starving limbs until, one by one, they fed the worms, never once approaching her home.

And her tears became flowers of ripe and pulsing blue.

"Let them come," she told the Woods. "Let him come to see my home."

Gathering her tear-flowers up, Gram took an earth-formed vase and called out to the kind-eyed wolf. With firm cries, she howled him home. Her voice pricked the ears of the gathering wolves. Ashamed, they slipped into the shade and left the smith alone.

Emboldened, the smith and his children spoke of wealth and immortality. They joked about the gold of Gramma Wolf. They laughed as the sun cut through the trees again, but their laughter held the edge of broken slate.

The kind-eyed wolf ran home to her, and he caught the family's secrets in his jaws. Those secrets turned to flowers as he ran. He dropped them at her doorway and called out to her. Gram let him in, gathered up those blood-bruise blossoms, and placed his flowers in the vase alongside her own. Watered, the flowers began to speak: about her son's treachery, his wife's ambitions, their children's selfishness, the plans they had for her in the house her husband built. She learned what the townsfolk said of her, heard the whispers of her wealth.

"Let them have it," she finally said. "Let them have it all."

Gram dashed the vase to the floor. The flowers scattered and went silent. Reaching for the wolf, Grandma melted into him. Wolf and woman became one, and Gramma Wolf ran off into the forest.

The family arrived just in time to see Gramma Wolf disappear beneath the trees. Finding nothing but a smashed vase, dying flowers and a lifeless cottage, they invented a tale of

Gramma-eating wolves when they returned home two days later, their sacks heavy with food and flowers and pillaged goods.

Lies breed lies, but Truth grows in fertile ground.

The girl who looked like a boy heard the whispers first. The blue flowers told her that she had been another man's child. She quarreled with her mother, who cut out the girl's tongue and pushed her down a well.

The youngest grandson heard the bruise-red flowers speak. They told him to cut open his eldest brother's throat. He did, and a diamond fell out. The boy grabbed the diamond and fled into the night.

The food they'd stolen turned to rust in their bellies. Their pots and pans crumbled into dirt. Bright leaves sprouted from their fingertips. The forge threw itself at the smith, shattering his legs and feet. Each night brought new whispers. Each day brought fresh calamities. The garden's night-blooming jarrowbanes, once deep blue, soon glowed with bright red spots. Curses flew and axes flashed. Only one of the woodsman's sons escaped alive, and he remained mute until his dying day.

Soon the townsfolk came and burned the old house to the ground.

Ash-white flowers grew in its dust.

Deep in the woods, Gramma Wolf still lives. Her two spirits transcend one flesh. To this day, she keeps a cottage near her waterfall, dancing in its garden each night. Since the old house burned, she has nothing to fear. Each spring, some folks say, she looks younger than she had the year before.

Townsfolk still visit her. They bring her goods from the marketplace. No one speaks of treasure anymore, and if they plot or gossip, they do so quietly. The wolves are listening, and the wind, and the flowers and the trees. Gramma Wolf no longer comes to town. The Old Woods speak her name.

If you follow the path past the ash-white grove, you may find the way to Gramma's house. Be careful where you step, and be kind to everything you meet. The forest watches, and it never forgets.

Near a waterfall, you may find her, dancing or brewing or tending her garden with the wolves. Her hair shines gray but her skin holds the freshness of youth. Even so, her eyes could match the stars for age. When she speaks, which is rare, her words sound smooth as polished wood. There's no iron in her home, nothing forged. Each tool and vessel has been shaped from earth or wood or skin or stone. Her hearth and kitchen hold the rich scent of trust.

Gramma Wolf brews heady mead, thick with the promise of everbursting spring. The vivid blooms of her garden are said to be among the finest found in any realm.

Just be truthful around them. You never know what they might say.

DRINKING
THE MOON

(For Sandi, who holds my heart.)

She was thirsty, they said, to drink the moon. She sighed like a forsaken queen and left her features bare. The young men painted their faces crimson, and powdered their chests with emerald dust. Still, she had eyes for none of them. Instead, each night the girl climbed the hill beyond their home, hushed whispers in her wake.

Her mother, it was said, had been an errant harvest wind that caressed a farmer boy to sleep. He had slumbered till the next full moon, when storms rattled the tall trees and brought some low and shuddering. As that storm-moon yielded to the sovereignty of day, the young man awakened in the healer's lodge, a bawling infant on his chest. He had raised her with tender strength until the night another storm came and carried him away. Since then, Wind's Daughter had subsisted on the kindness of her people, growing lean and beautiful as thunder.

Still, she thirsted, and not jhala-wine nor poppy syrup nor clear water fresh from the sky could slake that thirst.

Old Tor, whose laughter caused the ground to quake, mulled whip-grass into heady brews. She smiled as she drank them down, but shook her head with sorrow. Smiling Orishala, whose arms clattered with bright bangles marking favor in men's eyes, steamed wet earth from the dancing grounds, then mixed it with tears and washes of spring rain. The girl drank till her belly swelled above her skirts, but still the thirst remained. Each night, though, above her, the moon called out, sweet with glowing promise. *In me alone*, it seemed to call, *shall your thirst be fulfilled.*

And so, she sought to drink the moon.

On dark nights, when the sky-witch hid her face and the crops muttered restless in their beds, the girl tossed and turned on sweet-smelling grass and warm furs within the virgins' lodge. The other women watched her warily, their eyes dark with awe. No lullaby nor brew could bring her peace. Old Tor wove soft chains to bind her to her bed, but they broke apart on contact with her skin. Orishala, who knew about unruly sleep, sang ballads of warm water and old stone. Still, the girl rolled and sighed each night until moonlight shone again.

When moonlight bathed the landscape and made the lodge-roofs shine, the thirsty girl would slip past the brave eunuchs outside the virgins' door. Her cool touch upon their backs soothed them into sleep each night, and even the most steadfast among them could not resist that touch. Free to wander, she climbed the highest hill each night, picking through the wild darkness on feet light and sure as gold. Guided by the glow above, Wind's Daughter rose past tigers, wolves and serpents to reach the peak unharmed. There, upon the stark crown of that highest hill, she'd throw back her head and stretch up her arms and try to drink the moon.

But there are voids in heaven and emptiness on earth. Though her devotions held her still and silent through each night, the moon-glow could not soothe her thirst.

Each morning, as mists fled before the dawn, the girl returned to the lodge, heart-dulled and dusty-throated. Her eyes still shimmered with cold luminescence, but her touch was cool as autumn rain. Old Tor, then, would hold her as she wept; Orishala would brew her bale-herb tea and talk of lovers until the sun rose high. In time, Wind's Daughter would sleep, waking just before the skies blazed orange with the fading day. Returned – as was proper – to the virgins' lodge, she'd escape once more and try to drink that moon. It was enough to make wise men chew their beards, and maidens burn their braids and eat the ashes.

One morning, as she lowered aching arms and coughed to clear her dusty throat, Wind's Daughter wept, enraged. Her skin still rippled with the moon's cool touch, but her throat felt tinder-parched. In a flash of rage, she stamped her heel into the peak's bald head. A sudden arc of water burst across dry ground like rain. Within ten heartbeats, a spring ran down the hillside, chuckling to itself with riddles only water knows. Wind's Daughter bent to taste that stream, but it scourged her bitter throat. Fists clenched, she wandered down the hill toward home.

That dusk, as harsh winds swept the trees, the thirsty girl slipped once more through the doorway of the virgins' lodge. Once again, she ventured up the hillside, eyes luminous with unshed tears. And once again, she reached the peak, spread her arms, and threw her head back thirstily. Wind's Daughter opened her mouth wide, and crooned a wordless song so rich that fireflies rose from the woods below and danced around her, shining. The cool winds chilled her skin like stone and tossed her silky hair. Eyes closed, she reached out and up, as if to touch that moon.

At her feet, the water whispered. Its voice flowed across the silence of her calm. Finally, she opened her eyes, looked down, and saw the stream. And in its face, she saw the moon as well.

Bending down, she cupped her hands. Between them, moonlight swelled. Eyes open, she brought those waters to her lips. Wind's Daughter drank with eagerness, and down her throat slid the moon.

They say the sky-witch dimmed her light. Old Tor whispered that the wind-mother had come home. Orishala smiled and drew her lovers close. Amidst their furs and blankets, the people settled deeper into dreams. Children stilled to restful slumber. Old aches and pains faded; nightmares fled.

At the hilltop, Wind's Daughter drank the moon.

In morning, she descended, eyes shining, finally fulfilled. Those who saw her then said she left footprints of light. Mist embraced her as she walked.

And then, smiling, she faded and was gone.

AUTHOR'S NOTES

My primary childhood home was surrounded by woods.
Built in the late 1960s and early '70s, the development had been
constructed *within* the land, not *upon* the land. As a kid, I used to
spend uncountable hours in those woods – climbing trees, swinging
from vines, digging in creeks and shaping stories around my
surroundings. Later, as a teen and young adult, I'd run off to those
woods at all hours, sometimes in nothing but a pair of cutoffs and
my own sense of primal abandon. I'd bring girlfriends to the woods,
and we'd make out in the dirt or along the banks of forest creeks.
I felt a keen *belonging* in such places; when I connected with my
Pagan creed, its roots could literally be found in the woods where I
grew up.

Whenever I've needed to clear my head, I've headed off to the
woods or a beach. Thankfully, such places have always been close
to where I've lived. In later years, I learned long-distance hiking
from my friends Heidi and Kelly; those treks invested me with a
sense of the World Beyond the Cities, where you could dance in
a thunderstorm or wander through mists without seeing another
human being for days. Some injuries – none of them from hiking
– have limited my ability to do those sorts of things these days, but
the wilderness will always be a part of me, my faith, and the stories
I tell.

The Wild Girl has been a part of me for almost as long as the woods themselves. I've seen her run barefoot between the trees, sometimes in the flesh, often only in my mind's eye. I've been involved with some of her earthly manifestations too, but her true connection to me is internal. On a lot of levels, she is *me* – my Anima, or female aspect, tied eternally to primal Nature. These stories are hers, are mine, are beyond us both. I hope that you've enjoyed them too.

WAVES

Why must the Little Mermaid surrender to the loss of love? I envision her saying "*Fuck THAT noise!*" and using her superhuman powers to bring a world of hurt down on the kingdom and the man who spurned her. This tale began as a "sponsor award" for my first *Powerchords* book, and it seemed like a good way to start this collection off.

ELYNNE DRAGONCHILD

A milestone story for me, this tale took shape when I was working at "Virginia's Largest Shoe Store" – a job I loathed every second of the five years I spent there. Initially inspired by paintings from Rowena Morrell and Boris Vallejo, "Elynne" took shape across a collection of index cards I kept in my back pocket and wrote on when I had a chance. Liking what I saw, I transcribed my notes at home and then completed the story in a long day's push.

Polishing it up, I sent Elynne's saga in to Marion Zimmer Bradley… an editor who'd said she didn't want to see any more dragon stories unless they showed her something she'd never seen before. In her forward to the tale's appearance in *Sword & Sorceress*

IX, Marion wrote that "Phil seems to have thought the subject through, and brings us a different dragon story…" This tale became both my first attempted submission to a major publisher and my first mass-market sale. That victory encouraged me to keep writing; over 20 years after the story appeared, that's still my full-time career.

An amusing sidenote: Not long after I'd sold the story, I had sent a copy of it to my cousin John, a professional artist and lifetime fantasy fan. "It's kinda purple in places," John responded, "but you might be able to find a publisher for it somewhere." I laughed and said, "It's already been sold." "Well," he replied, "there you go then." He was right.

Even closer to home, my partner Sandi has said that she'd first encountered the story as a reader of the *Sword & Sorceress* series, back when the book originally appeared in the early '90s. "Huh," she recalls thinking, "A *guy* wrote this? I'll bet he'd be interesting to get to know." She got the chance a decade-and-a-half later, and didn't even realize that I'd written this particular story until we'd been going out for several months. Like I said, this tale's a milestone.

CHASER

Inspired by the implosion of my first marriage, crossed with an incident on a San Francisco beach in 1993, "Chaser" hits a familiar theme for me: The tension between a person's primal impulses and civilized behavior. As a Pagan, I can't stand to see people treat our environment carelessly, and being an avowed barefooter – someone who wears shoes as rarely as possible – I've got a special hatred for folks who smash glass all over the place.

During a visionquest on that San Francisco beach, I nearly stumbled into a discarded bonfire site in which some bunch of troglodytes had meticulously smashed Every. Single. Bottle they'd brought with them before leaving the whole shattered mess and the smoldering fire behind. Half in the spirit-world already (I was tripping on acid that evening, and the beach was wreathed in thick fog, as it always is during summer nights), I spent a seeming infinity choking down my rage as I sifted through the sand to pick out the shards of glass, metal cans, and paper waste. Thankfully, the assholes in question had left their beer-bags intact; by the bonfire's light, I put the wreckage into the bags and eventually cleaned up the site. I have no idea how long I was doing this, but it took quite a while. In the course of that clean-up, the task became a meditation. I had a lot of shit to work through that night, but the job gave me a much-needed focus. Like Rachel, I came to some conclusions that night that changed my life from then on out.

An early version of "Chaser," titled "Shards," appeared in two collections back during the 1990s. Because that tale was written as a work-for-hire piece based on White Wolf's *Werewolf: The Apocalypse* line, however, I didn't own the rights to it. This has always been a special story for me, though, so I rewrote "Shards" a few years back, taking out the shared-world elements, adding bits of my life since then to the piece, and making various other changes too. The revised tale is stronger and more personal than its original form, but its most personal elements – the wrenching choice, the broken glass, the end of one life and the acceptance of another – remain as vivid for me now as they were when I first lived that part of the story over 20 years ago.

WILLOW AND WIND

Back in early 2004, a bunch of us were touring to promote my new roleplaying game *Deliria: Faerie Tales for a New Millennium*. For me, that project offered a fresh start from my White Wolf Game Studio days, and I hit over a dozen conventions that year to bring it to the fans.

A few months earlier, I had encountered my close friend Kristen Leigh Elmore online; at a small convention, we met in person and clicked like mad. It wasn't a sexual connection but a bond of kindred spirits. She helped me run the first of many convention games that year... a story that I came up with the night before the con. "Willow and Wind" is based on my notes for that story: the tragic tale of Ariel – a restless wind-who-becomes-a-singer – and her lover Stickman, the tree-who-becomes-a-musician. Kristen and I, with two groups of players, ran wild with the story, taking it to emotional highs and lows that had folks literally in tears and cheering by the end.

A few months later, Kris and I – along with my then-business associates Kevin Divico and Burton Taylor – were planning to take the next portion of that story on the road to Dragon*Con at the end of our tour. Ariel would be doing a concert there; problem was, Kristen could not play the guitar. We were tossing around options when a tricky pixie with a huge grin and an even bigger guitar showed up at our booth to ask where she might find a place to play. We were at the FaerieWorlds festival, the pixie was SJ "Sooj" Tucker, and we were all looking at one of those life-changing encounters.

As with Kris, the bond was more or less instantaneous. I looked around for a place for Sooj and her two friends, but didn't find much worth working with. I had to return to our booth, so I asked

Kris to find a spot for them. She did so. About ten minutes later, she came back to the booth. "You *HAVE* to hear this," Kris told me.

"In a minute," I replied.

"*NOW*," she said, grabbing my sleeve and hauling me over to where Sooj and Company were set up and playing. When they'd finished the song they'd been playing, Kristen told Sooj to, "Sing me that song you just sang for me a minute ago." Sooj opened her mouth, and this *VOICE* boomed out – a swell of power and passion that left me speechless. We had found our Ariel. Sooj joined us a few weeks later in Atlanta, and we've been close friends ever since. Sooj even introduced me to Sandi – also at FaerieWorlds, three years later – so once again, a fantasy story laid the groundwork for real-life magic.

Seriously, this stuff is *POWERFUL.*

GRAMMA WOLF'S GARDEN

This one began as a flash-fiction intro to a shop presented in my book *Goblin Markets: The Glitter Trade*. It came pretty much from nowhere, but I enjoyed its inversion of the traditional Red Riding Hood dynamic and those images of whispering plants and the wolf-lover with flowers in his jaws. I'd submitted it to *Cabinet des Fées,* but the editors rightfully turned it down because it wasn't really a story quite yet. I expanded the fragment a year or so afterward, turning my Wild Girl archetype into a grown woman who really *does* run with the wolves.

Keeping the faerie-tale approach intact, I worked in themes of family dysfunction, unconventional relationships and domestic treachery. Beyond that, I integrated that sense of "bent time" you get when you walk away from all the usual landmarks of civilization. The wilderness operates on a different schedule than the industrial pace of our societies; in a vision I'd had years ago, Brother Crow referred to it as "crow time": the pace of Nature that couldn't care less about human concerns. Building the narrative around love, loss, "crow time" and elemental affinities, I turned "Gramma Wolf" from a vignette to a full-length story. When I read it aloud at HowlCon 2012, everyone wanted to know where they could find the story. A friend of mine wants to use it in a companion book she plans to do for an album she's recording, but this collection seemed like a "natural" place for Gram's tale, so it makes its debut here.

DRINKING THE MOON

Sometimes I tell bedtime stories to my lovers as they fade off to sleep. And generally, I forget those tales by morning. This one, though, stuck in my head, so I wrote it down the day after I'd told it to Sandi when we'd gone to bed. Shortly afterward, I sold it to *Cabinet des Fées*, where it became my first publication in that Journal of Fairy Tales. Like so many of my stories, it deals with someone outside the norm who finds her place in a greater world.

I guess we're all sorta looking for that place. And sometimes, when we're lucky and dedicated enough, we even find it.

May you always find your joy in a world that's big enough for you.

- Satyros Phil Brucato
Spring 2013

ABOUT THE AUTHOR

Satyros Phil Brucato gained the nickname "Satyr" back in the '90s for his passionate temperament, flirtatious ways, and work on the *Changeling: The Dreaming* RPG. Later, he was gifted with the slightly more dignified "Satyros" by his beloved tribe in Greece.

A professional author since the late '80s, Satyr's best-known for his short stories (in *Weird Tales, Sword & Sorceress, Cabinet des Fees*, and other publications); articles and columns (*Realms of Fantasy, newWitch, Witches & Pagans*, and other periodicals); comics (especially the webcomic *Arpeggio*); and RPG creations (*Mage: The Ascension, Deliria – Faerie Tales for a New Millennium, The Sorcerers Crusade*, and more).

He loves to hike, dance, play bass guitar, go barefoot, spin fire, and run around naked in the woods. Living in Seattle, WA, with his partner Sandra Damiana Buskirk, he can usually be found up to his eyeballs in four or five projects.

Connect with Satyros Phil Brucato online at:

Smashwords   www.smashwords.com/profile/view/quietthunder
Facebook   www.facebook.com/groups/126494504028229
Wordpress   satyrosphilbrucato.wordpress.com
Webcomic   www.arpeggiothecomic.com/episode1.htm

SNEAK PREVIEW

HOLY CREATURES
TO AND FRO

"Don't run off too far, Sarah," said my father. But I guess I did.

Sarah was me before I was Silk. I became Silk because Sarah couldn't run away.

I was four or five when my father took me walking to Woodside Park. It was just a few blocks away from home, but to me it felt like miles. There, rough concrete gave way to soft gray powder and chips of shredded wood. I swept out hieroglyphs with my toes, stomping up little clouds of dust. Despite sneaker-prints and an old mitten in the dirt, the park was empty save for us. At the far edge of it, down a long-sloped hill, a dark throat opened in the trees.

And I, of course, wanted to go down *that*.

The park itself sat dull and empty beneath a listless sky. There were swing-sets hung from cold gray pipes, and a slide that left brown smears across my butt and smelled like rust and old pee. I was bored out of my mind, I think, and my father probably was as well. I remember breathing sharp and prickly things when he picked me up. His barbwire scent burned the skin inside my nose and made me wriggle in his big, soft hands. After a few minutes swinging on the swings, and a few passes down that ugly slide, I spotted the path down into the woods. I wonder, now, if I knew what called to me.

Don't run off too far, Sarah, he said as I stepped into the shadows. If he'd only *known* how far I'd run someday...

After I'd whined a bit, my father relented and we walked hand-in-hand toward the forest mouth. Dim sunshine skittered on the rustling leaves. The green scents rising from that throat stirred primal ashes in me — memories, I think, of things I'd never seen. I remember even now how the soft grass beneath our feet gave way to prodding stones. "You see," my father said as I winced and grumbled. "You should have brought your shoes."

"*HATE* shoes," I probably replied. The lecture in his voice made me determined to prove him wrong. And so I pulled against his grip and led him down the path.

Things woke in me that day.

Cascades of treeleaf and fresh-turned earth greeted me as we descended. I felt them wash over me and down, as if the lights and scents and raw sensations of the earth became a cold, delicious waterfall. The trail wound serpentine through those violated woods, harvested from forest and salted with stone. Rainwash trickles cut through the soil, dryly displaying the course of water down the path. Roots cut their steps into the trail, dropping from packed earth to freefall in precarious instants. Shaped as it was by human hands, the path followed far more primitive designs.

I watched my arms as bands of twilight trickled down my skin. They blazed across the little hairs like falling stars, each bright magnificence a miracle. I breathed in the rich rot of fallen trees, the course tangle of underbrush and grass. The dull stab of gravel softened to a caress. Something dark and fluttering broke from the trees above our heads and clattered through the branches, an applause of leaves in its wake.

In hindsight, I'd found where my gods lived. That raw earth and devastating green became the temple I'd never known before.

We wandered for a while, lost moments that stretched in me like hours although I guess we lingered a few minutes at most. That first journey down the wooded path hangs in me like a frozen note of melancholy song.

I don't think we went far that day – less distance, as I'd later find, than I could walk on my own in a handful of minutes. Soon my father grunted at his watch and pulled me, protesting with sharp sounds, from the throat of that primeval grace. I felt the stones bite my sore feet as we left, as if to scold me for abandoning their path.

I went back there, though. Until the day I left home, I always returned. And most times later, I'd go alone…